Zombee A Go-Go

Rebecca M. Senese

Other Books by Rebecca M. Senese

A Very Zombie Christmas

The Beginners Guide to the Recently Deceased

The Night Killers

The In-Between Series
*Book 1: A Reluctance of Blood
*Book 2: A Remembrance of Flesh
*Book 3: A Retribution of Soul

Life Among the Dead: 5 Zombie Stories

Wreck the Halls: 5 Christmas Horror Stories

By Howl & Claw: 5 Werewolf Stories

With a Bite: 5 Vampire Tales

Bad Ends: 5 Horror Stories

In Dwarf Land and Cannibal Country

Daily Bread

The Color of Blood: The Chronicles of Richard Damon

*Forthcoming

Zombee A Go-Go

Rebecca M. Senese

RFAR Publishing
Toronto, Canada

Published 2013 by RFAR Publishing
Toronto, Canada
http://www.RFARPublishing.com

This is a work of fiction. All characters appearing in this work are fictitious. Any resemblance to real persons, living or dear is purely coincidental.

Trade paper edition designed by Rebecca M. Senese
in InDesign CS5.5

Electronic editions designed by Rebecca M. Senese

Cover design: Rebecca M. Senese
Image © Sanches1980 / Dreamstime.com

ISBN: 978-1-927603-09-3

Zombee A Go-Go

How they managed to keep the lights running without attracting free roaming hoards was something Jay always wondered whenever he visited the *Zombee A Go-Go*. The large building had been a new car showroom once upon a time before everything went to hell. Now the huge expanse of windows had been boarded up and decorated with peeling black paint and yellow letters that blazed out *Zombee A Go-Go*. From the flat roof, a spotlight beamed into the sky, rotating in jerking circles, a beacon to travelers from miles around. Whenever he was nearby, Jay stopped for a meal and a beer, and to marvel at the place's continued existence.

This time he arrived before sunset, kicking the dirt off his boots before passing through the decontamination unit installed at the front entrance. No one got in without decontamination. Must be a pain in the ass for the employees, but then again they probably appreciated the clean bill of health on a daily basis. Not much chance of getting that in the surrounding area.

Maggie the waitress nodded at him as she approached, wiping her hands on a dish towel that hung in front of the yellowing apron tied around her waist. Even the red and white uniform looked faded. "Just you today, Jay?"

"Just me, Maggie. How are things going?"

"Same old," she said and steered him toward a table near the wall by the back exit like he favored. Like most wranglers, he preferred having an easy exit and a wall to his back in case of trouble.

He slipped off his long battered leather coat and slung it over the opposite chair before he sat down. He rolled up the sleeves of his shirt and brushed a few strays piece of dirt from his jeans.

"Had a ruckus the other night. Darren and Big Bill got into it. Murdock had to boot them both out by ten." Maggie swiped at the stained table top with her towel.

"Darren and Big Bill?" Jay said. "That doesn't sound right. They've been best friends for years."

Maggie shrugged. "Don't seem that way any longer. Want a beer?"

"Yeah, bring me a pint."

She dropped a coaster in front of him and ambled off, wiping at the empty tables as she passed. Still early, only a few of the tables had patrons clustered around them, mostly older folks and a few youngsters who didn't look old enough to be there. Not like anyone enforced the liquor laws anymore. Be a long time before that mattered again, if ever. Maybe if infection or mutation or whatever it was died down and wranglers like himself could get a better hold on the zombie population, then maybe society would have a chance to get annoying and rule laden again. Until then they squeaked by.

Maggie returned with his beer and a menu. Jay ordered the stew.

As she headed back to the kitchen, Jay spotted Murdock across the room. He wore his customary black pants and black shirt, left open around his thick neck. He rounded the raised stage with the catwalk, moving with a smoothness surprising for a man of his bulk. But Jay knew there was muscle beneath those layers of fat. Murdock surveyed the room as he walked across it. Dim light reflected off his bald head. When he spotted Jay, he nodded and changed direction, moving toward his table.

"Evening, Jay. You're here early." He held out a meaty hand.

Jay shook his hand. "Finished up a job at the Witiker farm earlier today. I want to head out early tomorrow so I thought I'd get in before the rush."

A smile crossed Murdock's craggy face. "You may want to stick around until a bit later."

"Oh?"

"Got an interesting show. Been getting lots of notice." He flipped the menu over and tapped at the sheet taped to the back. *Melanie and the Zombies - see the renowned Zombie Tamer.*

Jay snorted. "Zombie tamer, ain't no such thing."

Murdock's smile got bigger. "You should see it before you judge."

Jay tapped the price printed beneath the notice. "A little rich for my blood."

"Seeing as you're a wrangler, you're my guest," Murdock said. "See how she does it." The smile faded. "Might be of use to you."

Before Jay could question him, Murdock turned away, slipping past the tables toward the bar. Just then Maggie returned with the stew and set it in front of Jay. The rich smell of spices distracted him and he began to eat.

As usual, the warm stew hit the spot after weeks of cold rations. Jay savored every bite, setting the fork down between each as he chewed. By the time he finished, half the tables were full and a steady flow of people passed through the decontamination unit. Jay checked his watch. Only eight o'clock, still two hours before the first show. He watched as two men got into a whispered argument over a table close to the left of the stage. Before it came to blows, two of Murdock's bouncers waded forward, grabbing both and dragging them away. Another man pounced on the table.

From his vantage point by the wall, Jay studied the odd behavior. It hadn't been like this the last time he'd visited the *Zombee A*

Go-Go. He fingered the notice on the back of the menu as he took a sip of his beer. Maybe he should stick around.

After the stew, he indulged in a piece of apple pie and another beer. Unheard of luxuries but it gave him more of an excuse to stay.

By nine thirty, the place was packed with more jostling for position along the bar. From the corner, Murdock grinned and gave Jay a thumbs-up. Even Maggie, normally bland and professional, smiled and joked with customers. Jay saw her stuffing bills into her pockets. Her smile got wider.

Guess this show was a boost for everyone.

At ten o'clock, a hush fell over the crowd. The main lights dimmed and a harsh white spotlight flashed onto the faded red curtain at the back of the stage. Jay waited, hand resting around his beer glass.

Nothing.

He waited.

Still nothing.

The crowd seemed poised in expectation. Jay frowned, glancing at the eager faces. Even Murdock stared at the stage.

Nothing.

The curtain parted. Figures ran across the stage, heading for the audience. Garbled snarls sounded. Wild zombies! Unmuzzled and unchained, they jumped down from the stage, reaching for the first tables, hands out in jagged claws.

Jay was already on his feet, length of chain in his hand, moving forward, ready to swing...

"Halt!"

A woman appeared in the center of the stage, right arm held up, fingers spread wide. The zombies froze, hands inches from the patrons, who were leaning away.

The woman lowered her arm until it rested at her side. "Return."

The zombies backed away in jerking motions, as if the movement was not of their will. Each turned and crawled back onto the stage. As they approached the woman, she pointed at the spot in front of her. The zombies congregated there and sat at her feet. Jay counted five in all.

"Seat yourself, wrangler," the woman said from the stage. "We have no need of your skill here."

A chuckle rumbled through the crowd. Jay became aware that he stood next to the stage, chain still clutched in his hand held at the ready. He took another look at the zombies sitting at her feet then backed away to his table by the wall. Maggie stood next to it, grinning as he sat down. Across the room, he saw Murdock's wide smile.

Jay kept the chain in hand at the ready.

Neat trick, but those zombies could turn at any moment.

"I am Melanie the zombie tamer," the woman said. "You may think this is a trick, these aren't real zombies or maybe they're only partly turned. But I can tame any zombie, any time. And I'll start now!"

She gestured away from the zombies with both hands. They shambled off toward the sides of the stage. Gloved hands reached out from back stage to grab hold of the zombie arms and drag them off.

Probably kept them caged back stage, Jay thought as he studied the woman. Even from here, she was short. Maybe five feet even with the high-heeled boots. Dark hair surrounded her narrow, unlined face, tumbled over her shoulders and down her back. A black leather mini skirt slung low on her hips and the sleeveless top showed off well-toned arms. She had the athletic build that Jay preferred over the usually heavy bosomed dancers Murdock employed. He clenched the chain, trying to keep his mind on business.

Melanie snapped her fingers toward the right side of the stage. From behind the curtain, two men pushed a cage on stage.

Inside, a large male zombie slapped at the reinforced acrylic sides. One of the men stepped forward and Jay recognized his face although he didn't know the man's name.

"I help run the Braedon farm five miles south," the man said. "We caught this zombie just yesterday. It's been kept in this cage all this time."

"I've never seen him before," Melanie said. "You can testify to that."

"I sure can, ma'am," said the man.

She nodded at him and smiled. "Open the cage."

The man hesitated. Even from where he sat, Jay saw the man's brow draw down. Jeers came from the audience.

"It's all right." Melanie held out her hands to still the crowd. Silence flowed across them. "Open the cage," she said again.

He shook his head but reached for the latch. The other man held out a two pronged prod, the ends crackling with electricity. As the latch dropped down, both men jumped back.

The zombie swatted at the sides of the cage. When it hit the door, it jostled, shifting open an inch. The zombie roared and pounded harder. The door sprang open and the zombie lurched out.

It hesitated a moment as if startled by its new freedom, then with a howl it lunged toward Melanie. Two feet away, one foot... Jay jumped to his feet...

"Stop."

Her musical voice spoke the single word at normal volume but it carried through the breathless silence in the room. The zombie managed a half step before it stopped. Hands in front of Melanie's face clenched and unclenched did not move closer.

"Hands down," she said.

The hands stayed in position, clenching and unclenching. The zombie began a chewing motion, mouth opening and closing almost in time to his hand movements.

Even from where he stood, he saw the slight frown on the woman's face. Her head dipped as she stared at the zombie.

"Hands down!"

Another moment, then the zombie's hands lowered in jerking movements. The mouth continued its chewing motion. A scattering of applause started around the room. Melanie turned to face the audience, a smile blossoming on her face. She bowed but Jay noticed the sweat on her brow.

He didn't think it was from the spotlight.

She performed several more tricks, having the zombie sit in a chair, pretend to eat with utensils, brought out another zombie and had them throw a ball back and forth. They missed catching the ball more often than not and she just handed them another ball.

The exhibition continued for half an hour before she finished to a standing ovation.

Jay stayed seated as the crowd roared its approval and then settled down to drink. Music blared from the speakers, sounding tinny with too much bass as the first of the buxom dancers appeared on stage, dressed in a strategically tattered costume. She lurched around the stage, pretending to be a zombie as the music pounded away.

"What you think?" Murdock's voice cut through the music. He pulled out a chair and sat down at the table across from Jay.

"Interesting act," Jay said. "What's her gimmick?"

"No gimmick. She can tame zombies. I've seen her do it to several at a time."

"She seemed to have a little trouble with the first one."

Murdock waved off his skepticism. "Jitters. She knew there was a wrangler in the audience, made her a little nervous."

Jay tilted his head, studying Murdock's eager expression. "Why you pushing so hard, wondering what I think? What's going on?"

Murdock blinked. A look of innocence flashed onto his face. He held up his hands. "Nothing's going on."

Jay drained the last of his beer. "Right. Then I'd best be getting gone. Have an early start tomorrow."

He started to stand but Murdock's beefy hand grabbed his arm.

"Wait, Jay." The big man's shoulders drooped. "Okay, I do want a favor."

Jay sat down and leaned back in his chair, crossing his arms over his chest. He kept a stern look on his weathered face.

"What's that, Murdock?"

Murdock shook his head, almost as if he couldn't believe he was saying the words. "Melanie wants to learn wrangling."

A guffaw burst from Jay's lips before he could stop it. He clamped his mouth shut to stop the noise. Around him, no one noticed, focused as they were on the woman gyrating on stage to the music.

"You can't be serious," Jay said.

Murdock shrugged. "It's not my idea."

"No, it's mine."

Her voice cut through the wave of music and cheering crowd as if it was a bullet aimed at Jay's head. He turned and she stood half a table away, arms crossed over her chest. She'd changed out of the mini skirt and sleeveless top into a pair of heavy pants and long sleeved shirt. Her dark hair had been pulled back into a pony tail that hung down her back, a suggestion of the tumbling waves from before.

"Ma'am," Jay said. "You have a mighty fine act."

She stepped closer to the table, standing by Murdock's shoulder facing Jay.

"That's all you think it is though. An act."

"I think things can be a lot more easily handled on a stage than out in the country."

"Where do you think I first got started?"

Her voice snapped at him. She was really angry and not hiding it well. Jay pushed his chair back and stood up. He touched the brim of his hat.

"Good night, ma'am."

Before she spoke again, he picked up his coat, slung it over his arm then turned and moved away, heading to the entrance. As he passed the bar, he dropped some bills on Maggie's tray and wished her a good night.

Through the doors, the night held a crisp bite in the air. A light breeze nipped at his arms. He slipped on the coat, careful that the only sound was the hiss of the soft leather. He hadn't planned to be out this late. He hurried to distance himself from the blazing light of the *Zombee A Go-Go* without making too much noise. You never knew which would attract a zombie more, light or noise.

Then he heard footsteps behind him. Not the shambling, arrhythmic, hurrying kind a zombie would make. A person was following him.

No, not a person. An idiot.

He turned and it was Melanie, as he'd suspected. She paused when he turned then continued forward to meet him.

"I wanted to talk to you," she said. "I didn't get a chance since you hurried out of the bar."

"So you decide to show just how little you know about zombies and follow me outside to have a conversation." He kept his voice low.

Her back stiffened. "You think I don't know the danger? I've been around zombies my whole life!" He'd made her furious but at least she enough sense to drop the volume of her voice.

"You would never know it from the way you're acting."

"If you'd bothered to stay inside, we could have had this conversation there." She jerked a thumb back at *Zombee A Go-Go*. "You're the one who walked out."

Even in the dim light, he could see the color rise on her cheeks, sending an alluring blush down her neck, under the collar of her shirt. He blinked to distract himself. It wouldn't do to let his mind wander out here no matter how attractive the distraction.

"Fair enough," he said. "We'll discuss it in my truck but you'll not change my mind."

He turned and moved on again, using his usual quiet, sliding motion. From behind, he heard her following, her steps now sliding in random patterns as well. Well, at least she seemed to know something about walking outside in the wild.

At the side of his truck, he unlocked the door to the back cabin and motioned her in. She slid up and in, moving past him. He caught a brief whiff of soap. He inhaled, catching a touch of her scent beneath it. Even the soap smelled exotic these days.

Damn, he'd been out too long to let her turn his head this way. Should have had this talk in the bar after all. Too late now. He climbed in and closed the door.

Even though he'd sealed every window and crack against light spillage, he kept the lighting in the back to a bare minimum. Normally it didn't matter. He knew this place like the back of his hand but now with another person in the cabin, it felt small and claustrophobic. He couldn't take the big stride into the center like he wanted.

"Have a seat." He gestured to the narrow couch along the wall, the one that pulled out into his sleeping cot. She sat, turning her legs to the side to let him move past. He reached the back cupboard and pulled out a couple of glasses and a bottle of bourbon. He inclined it toward her and she nodded. He splashed some in each glass and handed one to her.

The bottle went back into the cupboard before he took a sip. Out in the open he only allowed himself one drink a night. You never knew when a hoard was going to turn up.

She waited until he took a sip before she drank. Maybe she did know a thing or two about outside since she seemed to have some manners if not much sense.

He watched the movement of her throat as she swallowed. She'd taken a nice hefty sip and no coughing. Lady knew her bourbon. Keep thinking that way. It was a good distraction instead of noticing the softness of her skin. He forced his gaze to his own glass.

Been out in the wild too long.

"Murdock said you were the best wrangler in this area," she said. "I want to learn from the best."

Jay snorted and took his own swallow. The burning liquid seared his throat as it went down. After the two beers, it created a pleasant buzz.

"Ma'am, as I said there's a big difference between the stage and the open country."

"And I said where do you think I learned to do what I do?"

"Then why do you need me?" he said. "You got that taming down, why not use that?"

She shifted in her seat, setting her glass down on the small counter beside the couch. The glass reflected the rusting chrome from the surface. Jay focused on that, ignoring the way her shirt tugged around her front, outlining the curves of her breasts.

Damn, out in the wild way too long.

"I can only tame a few at a time," she said. "It takes all my concentration. If I learn to wrangle, maybe I can increase my range, tame larger groups. Maybe we can make zombies productive."

"We?"

She frowned. The way her forehead puckered in the center between her perfect eyebrows made his mouth go dry. He sipped more bourbon. Thank god for that burning down his throat.

"I realize I can't do it all myself," she said. "I'd be willing to take on a partner."

He almost choked on his laugh.

Now her frown straightened into a glare of anger. Her body stiffened. Her hands clenched themselves on her lap. Even in the dim light, he could see the flush of color on her cheeks and the way it spread down her neck to disappear under her shirt. He wondered how far down that color spread.

He pulled his focus back to his glass again, stifling his laughter. It wouldn't do to make too much noise out here.

"You don't have to be insulting," she said.

"I wouldn't be if you had sense in your head," he said. "You do some fine talking but all I've seen are parlor tricks up on a stage. It's different out in the wild."

"So why don't you take me out there?" she said. "You're so sure I can't handle it, why don't you prove it? If I last a day, you'll train me."

"This isn't a game," he said. "I'm not gonna take you out there just to prove a point. You ain't just risking yourself, you risk me and anyone else you might even meet. Zombie herds can have territories hundreds of miles across. There's lots of settlements and small homes in there. No telling who you might hurt if you get turned. Then that's on me for being stupid enough to take you out." He shook his head, setting his glass down on the counter beside him. "No, ma'm, I ain't doing it."

"But..."

He held up his hand. "Don't bother wasting your breath."

"You won't even talk about it?"

"We've talked enough." He stood up, stooping so he didn't hit his head on the roof. The dim interior of the cabin seemed to sway a little, or maybe it was him. It had been a long time since he'd had so much to drink at one time. Not the smartest thing to do out here.

"I'll walk you back to the *Go-Go*," he said.

She stood up and pushed past him. He caught the warm scent of her skin as she brushed against his arm.

"Don't bother," she said. "I know the way."

Before he could stop her, she hurried down the three steps and was out the door.

She clicked it shut behind her. He followed to the closed door and pulled the curtain aside to watch. She moved with the arrhythmic shuffle walk to avoid attracting zombies. She headed for the door to the *Zombee A Go-Go*.

He sagged against the doorframe. Maybe that'd get that fool notion out of her head. Wanting to be a wrangler, what nonsense. He pulled his coat off as he moved back into the deeper part of the cabin. Funny that it still seemed small even without her. He hung up the coat and moved back to take care of the glasses. When he reached the spot where she'd sat, he could still smell the soft musk of her skin. Without thinking, his hand reached down to the spot on the thin couch where she'd sat. He could almost feel the warmth of her there.

It'd been too long since he'd had anyone inside his cabin. Maybe he shoulda poured her another drink. Who knew what might have happened?

Then she mighta talked him into this wrangler nonsense.

He shook his head. Probably best she left.

Now he could just go on with his life.

First chance he got tomorrow, he'd air out this cabin, get rid of her warm, sexy scent.

He woke up with a dry mouth and a pounding headache. Who woulda thought two beers and a bourbon could do that? Man, he must be getting old. He lurched up out of the pullout bed in his cabin and stumbled forward to the small sink opposite the door. He splashed out some water from a jug and rubbed it into his face. That helped take some of the gummy feeling from his eyes. He grabbed a towel and dried his face.

Most mornings, he shaved. He knew it seemed silly, especially in the wild country. Who was to care whether he had a beard or not, but his momma always said a civilized man kept a smooth face. Today he didn't feel so civilized so he skipped it. Momma would understand even if she would frown about it.

He used the rest of the water for a quick standing wash, using an old rag to rub all over his body. Then he dressed in a fresh shirt and pair of jeans. He hadn't planned to stick around today but seeing as he'd overdone it, maybe he'd see about doing some laundry here. Surely Murdock would let him use the tubs for a price. Maybe Jay'd even splurge and have a warm breakfast.

The sun was already blazing in the sky when he stepped out of his trailer. It started his headache pounding even stronger in his temples. Jay squinted as he headed for the front door of the *Zombee A Go-Go*. His usual sliding step seemed a little rougher this morning.

Damn, he was getting old.

At the front door, the early shift let him in,

and he passed through decontamination with ease. Like most outfits, the *Zombee A Go-Go* ran practically twenty-four seven, catering to different clientele during different hours. This morning, Jay noticed several farmers scattered around, sharing breakfast while negotiating deals. He himself had gathered a few contracts in the early mornings here. But right now, he just wanted coffee.

Bertha, the morning waitress, appeared and waved him to a table just one over from the one he sat in last night. It was an odd sort of déjà vu except Bertha was no Maggie. Tall and thin, with brown frazzled hair in a cloud around her narrow face, the red and white uniform hung on her like it was two sized too big. Bertha's arms were so thin, Jay thought he could snap them like a twig but he'd seen her handle a huge tray laden with heavy food.

"I'll have the big breakfast with coffee," he said. "Lots of coffee."

"Coffee," Bertha said. She nodded and

turned away, hurrying to deliver his order to the back.

Jay leaned back in his chair, listening to the squeak of the wood beneath him. Even through the dull sheen on the table top, dotted with multiple rings from old drinks, he couldn't feel a tad of stickiness. Murdock ran a clean shop, that was for sure.

Another sign of a civilized man. Jay knew his momma would have approved of this place, even if she didn't much like the evening fare.

Footsteps moving closer made him look up, expecting to see Bertha returning with a fresh pot of coffee. Instead it was Murdock towering over his table. A frown stretched across his face. He wore the same black shirt and black pants, or very similar ones.

"What are you doing here?" Murdock said.

"Having breakfast," Jay said. "Thought I'd splurge. Maybe do some laundry if you let me rent some time with your tubs."

The frown on Murdock's face deepened, the lines creasing in the folds of his skin around his mouth and along his expanse of forehead stretching almost over the top of his bald head.

"I thought you took Melanie out for wrangling this morning."

A tiny niggling alarm started in the pit of Jay's stomach, forcing him to sit straighter in the chair. The old wood groaned under his movement.

"I told her I wouldn't do it. I sent her back here last night. She didn't return?"

Murdock's beefy hand grabbed the back of the chair opposite Jay and wrenched it back. He dropped his big body into it and leaned across the table, thick hands flat against the smooth tabletop.

"Let me get this straight," Murdock said. "You said no to her and sent her back here?"

Jay nodded. "That's right."

Murdock's lips thinned. "She didn't come back in last night."

The niggling alarm flared higher. "I don't know what happened to her."

"What do you mean you don't know what happened to her?" Murdock's temper flared, sending his voice booming through the room. Silence dropped over the other tables. All heads turned to watch them.

"You didn't walk her back?" Murdock said.

"I offered," Jay said. "She refused." His voice trailed off. He remembered the flash of anger in her eyes, the haughty refusal. He'd stupidly listened to her and let her go outside in the dark.

Alone.

From the look on Murdock's face, Jay knew he was thinking the same thing.

How could he have done that? Been so stupid?

"I didn't see any trace of attack outside." Jay's words tumbled out fast as if trying to beat each other out of his mouth. "I didn't hear any zombies after she left. They aren't known for being stealthy and she was moving the right way, with the sliding, stopping motion."

"I don't care how she was walking," Murdock said. "You let her go by herself. Now who knows where she's gone?" One large hand shot up, fingers curling back in a fist. One finger stuck out at him.

"I blame you for this. If anything happened to her…"

"'cuse me, Murdock." A thin voice off to the right interrupted Murdock's flow. Jay glanced over.

A short farmer stood in faded but clean overalls. He wore a white shirt under them, the cuffs buttoned at his wrists. He held his hat in his hands, the way he twisted the brim with his weathered hands the only evidence of his nerves. He held his gaze steady on Murdock and his voice didn't quiver.

"You'all talkin' about that lovely lady from last night?" the farmer said.

"Yes, I am, Wayne," Murdock said. "What of it?"

"I saw her early this morning on my way here," the farmer said. "She was traveling with Thrifty Morris."

Now the feeling of alarm in Jay's belly was buzzing full out. Opposite him, Murdock straightened away from him, staring at the thin farmer.

"When was this?" he said.

"Early," Wayne said. "The sun was just comin' up. I was maybe halfway here, out along Old Mill Road."

"Thrifty Morris." Murdock spat the words out. "That piece of trash. This is your fault, Jay."

"My fault?"

"I asked you for a favor."

"You asked me to listen to her. I listened. She don't have no business trying to be a wrangler."

"I didn't ask your opinion." Murdock's finger stabbed out at Jay again. This time Jay noticed the tremor in it. "You're going to find her."

"What?"

"Find her and bring her back," Murdock said. "If you don't, you'll never be welcome here again and I'll see to it the word spreads. You'll find you won't be welcome anywhere within five hundred miles of here."

"Murdock..."

"I mean it, Jay! You get my niece back or what you've got in your truck is the last stock you'll ever have!"

Niece? Oh shit.

Jay stood up, pushing back his chair just as Bertha arrived with his coffee. He grabbed the cup from her hand and slung back the hot liquid. The bitter brew burned on the way down but brought a sharp clarity to his mind. He set the cup down on the table.

"Cancel my breakfast, Bertha, I got some place to be."

"Make sure you aren't returning alone," Murdock said. The warning in his voice was plain.

Jay nodded, touched the brim of his hat to Bertha and slipped out of the *Zombee A Go-Go.*

So much for an easy start to the day.

Even with his sunglasses, the glare from the bleached pavement in front of him made Jay's head pound. He swallowed a gulp of water and set the bottle back in the cup holder beside him in the truck. He'd unlatched the trailer and left it back at the *Zombee A Go-Go*. It was faster traveling in just the pickup.

Without the balancing weight of the trailer, the pickup jostled on uneven pavement that was as cracked and grey as some old women he'd seen. Around him, the parched land covered with brush and twisted bushes stretched out away for miles. Most of the farmers were further inland, closer to the smaller lakes and rivers for irrigation. A few drove livestock along here but this wild country made it a challenge to keep them free from zombie attacks. Thrifty Morris made his living defending some of the livestock farmers, and not doing a very good job of it, so Jay had heard.

Had Melanie gone through all the wranglers at the *Go-Go* last night before she got a yes from Thrifty? She must have been mighty desperate to accept Thrifty's help.

Murdock shoulda told him she was his niece. Jay woulda accepted her then. But that wasn't Murdock's way and from what he'd see of Melanie, he couldn't imagine her wanting any special treatment either. So instead she hooked up with some idiot who barely managed to keep his hide intact, never mind look after another person.

There was a reason most wranglers worked alone, and a reason why Thrifty Morris did that for sure. He'd never be able to look after her and wrangle any zombies that happened around. Thrifty could barely manage to walk and breathe at the same time.

Jay hit the edge of his palm on the steering wheel as he sped along, the truck spitting up clouds of dust behind him. The dust seeped in through the cracks along the top of his window and gummed up his eyes, making his nose itch. He even tasted it in the back of his throat no matter how much water he drank. It didn't matter how long he'd been out here, he still wasn't used to the scratchiness at the back of his throat.

Damn, he never shoulda let her leave the trailer. If he'd known she was Murdock's niece... Shoulda offered her another drink, been a little nicer. Who knew where things mighta gone then? Of course, that might not be any better. He'd still be facing Murdock's wrath.

Facing zombies might just be a better option.

He glanced at the map resting on the passenger's seat beside him. It flapped against the edges of the gun holding it down. He was coming up to Alder's Mount on the left, a black scar of a hill rising out of the desert floor like a sore. According to the map, it was another mile straight and then right, toward Hillard's farm. Word at the *Go-Go* had been that Thrifty had a contract out this way. Jay couldn't know for sure this was where Thrifty was headed, but Wayne's farm was five miles further along this road and he'd seen Thrifty coming this way. It was as good a bet as any.

The mile came up fast. Jay took the right onto a dirt road. For all the annoyance of the cracked pavement, he immediately missed it as soon as he'd traveled a few feet on the dirt road. Pot holes six inches deep dotted the trail. The pickup groaned and jostled as it bounced from one hole to the next. He found he had to cut speed in half, and then half again, just to stop from whacking his head on the roof of the cab.

His body tensed. He clutched the steering wheel. This had to be the worst road he'd ever driven on. He glanced to either side. The desert didn't look much more enticing either.

Finally in the distance, he caught sight of a dot off to the left. As he bounced closer, it became a structure. Bouncing closer still, he saw it was an old farm house, listing to the left, all color bleached off the walls until they were almost the same beige color as the sand around it. Even the tiled roof was bleached of color but looked otherwise intact. As he approached, he saw an irregular fence of wire and wood stretching out behind the house.

Farther out in the field, another taller structure stretched out, this one more fortified. A white barn with stronger, sturdier walls and heaps of rock and rubble piled along the bottom of the walls to discourage zombies. Thick double wooden doors, closed but with no exterior lock. Two fences surrounded the barn, the wire twisted and doubled back on itself, another defense. Good ones. Anything that discouraged and confused zombies worked well. After a time, the zombies would move away, head for something easier.

Like the house.

He turned into the path leading to the house. No one emerged from within. Strange. His truck engine would be easy to hear for miles in this quiet morning. He stopped and turned off the truck. The engine ticked as it cooled. Jay grabbed his hat and shoved it on his head, pulling the wide brim over his eyes. Then he scooped up the gun and left the truck.

He circled around the house, looking for any sign of life. Nothing stirred inside.

He stepped closer, lifting the sunglasses off his eyes. As he stepped into the shadow created by the listing structure, he could see the windows had been shattered. Only a few jagged shards stuck in the frames. Glass ground to dust glinted on the porch.

He snapped the safety off the gun before he

stepped onto the stairs leading to the porch and the front door. A breeze came up, tossing dust and rattling the door in its frame.

Pointing the gun down, Jay reached for the door. The knob turned in his hand.

The door creaked open.

The smell of dust floated out. He inched through the door frame, keeping his back against the door to hold it open. After the bright sunshine, it took time for his eyes to adjust, then he remembered he was still wearing the sun glasses.

He flicked them up on his forehead and peered around.

Deserted.

Empty rooms spread out through the house. From the front door, he could see into the living room off to the right and a second smaller room off to the left. Even the stairs leading upward had an air of decay and abandonment. Dust and dirt piled in small drifts up each stair. He saw sand spread across the floors, piling against the floorboards. In the living room, the floor sagged toward the window as if it would soon collapse downward.

No one lived in this house.

So where were they? This had to be Hillard's farm. Where was Hillard and his family?

He backed out of the house, letting the door swing shut. Facing the bright sunshine again, he flicked his glasses back across his eyes, then took a two handed grip on his gun. This was weird, and Jay did not like weird. Life was weird enough just dealing with zombies.

He caught sight of the barn again. Fortified yet some distance from the house, maybe fifty yards.

Had Hillard made the decision to let the zombies take the house?

Jay jogged down the porch to his truck. The area looked clear. Other than the house and the barn, there wasn't much in terms of coverage for at least a few fields' length.

If he'd been feeling better, he would have taken the truck but the idea of climbing back in and then out again just for a few yards' travel made his headache even more. Instead, he pulled out his satchel with a few extra clips and headed over to the barn.

When he reached the door, he noticed the camera high above him, well out of reach of even the tallest zombie. They would have had to climb up three high to reach it and zombies weren't known for their reasoning abilities. Nor did Jay know of any animals who used a camera at the front of their barn.

Before he could raise a hand to knock, the right door creaked open. The figure of a man stood just inside, hidden by the darkness.

"What do you want?" he said.

"I'm a wrangler," Jay said. "Name's Jay. Murdock from the *Go-Go* asked me to fetch his niece Melanie. She was headed to the Hillard farm with Thrifty Morris. Are you Hillard?"

The man pulled the door open enough for him to step out. In the sunshine, he stood just an inch under Jay's six three. Short brown hair sported on his round head. His skin was weathered and brown. He wore a dark t-shirt and neat overalls tucked into worn leather boots. He pulled a white kerchief from his pocket and passed it over his forehead.

"I'm Hillard," he said. "I hired Thrifty Morris to get rid of a herd of zombies out yonder."

He pointed away from the house toward the distant hills that rose up like smeared watercolors against the sky.

"How big is the herd?" Jay asked.

"Dunno," Hillard said. "They been harassing us for months. We tried everything, even moved out here because the barn is stronger than the house. They rampaged through six weeks ago, wretched everything."

Jay nodded. A lot of damage from six weeks ago.

"They keep coming back. First time we tried to go back to the house but they came again. Now we don't even bother. Safer out here until we can get rid of that herd."

"So you hired Thrifty?"

Hillard shrugged. "The only one who'd take credit. Can't bring in the crops or let out our animals with all those zombies around."

"Sorry to hear that, Mr. Hillard."

A frown formed on the farmer's face. "I got a contract with Morris. He don't get paid til those zombies are gone."

"I'm not here for Thrifty," Jay said. "Just Murdock's niece."

"Murdock ain't got no pull out here," Hillard said. "I got a contract."

Jay held up his hands, letting his gun swing easy. "I'm not interfering in your contract..."

"If Morris brings an assistant, that's included in our contract, says it on page two. I don't care if she is Murdock's niece, she's part of my contract and ain't going back til those zombies are gone."

Damnit, Hillard would stand on principle. Out here in the wild, squelching on a zombie contract was a killing offence. No one backed out without good reason. Not even a crap wrangler like Thrifty Morris. But as long as he killed some of the zombies, that should be good enough to fulfill the contract.

"I'll make sure he gets 'em," Jay said.

"All of 'em," Hillard said. "The whole herd. It's in the contract."

"Thrifty wouldn't have signed on for that."

Hillard nodded. "He did. I offered double and a share in my hogs. I got my own contracts to fill if I can just get rid of the damned zombies. Then I'll have plenty to spare."

The farmer dug in his pocket and pulled out several folded pieces of paper. He held them out to Jay.

"See on page two."

Jay took the contract and skimmed through it. Sure enough, the clause on page two covered any assistants and laid out the bonus specification of double plus shares upon destruction of the zombie herd.

Thrifty musta been out of his mind to sign this, or desperate.

Now he'd taken Murdock's niece into that mess.

And Jay was gonna have to follow.

Damnit.

He handed the contract back to Hillard. "Can you tell me the direction they headed in?"

Hillard stuffed the contract into his pocket. "Why you wanna know that?"

Jay sighed. "I'm another of Thrifty's assistants."

He headed off toward the fields, following the rutted path Hillard pointed out. A few clouds had rolled in, giving some relief from the unrelenting sun and casting darkening shadows across the desert floor. As he drove toward the distant mountains, the landscape became more choppy. The ruts were deeper and more uneven, causing the truck to bounce hard, smacking his tail bone over and over. He'd be bruised before long but it wasn't the first time. He was more worried about the truck's shocks.

Sometimes he wished he had a horse, even if they weren't much use against zombies.

Zombies were just as happy to devour a horse as a person. Jay couldn't bear the thought of leading a poor horse into that situation on purpose, although he knew of wranglers who didn't discriminate.

They weren't much better than zombies, as far as he was concerned.

The brush along either side of the path thickened, the leaves a mottled mix of green, yellow, and brown with an equal dose of nasty looking thorns sticking out among the leaves. Desert thistle, he always called them, though he didn't know their name for sure. He wasn't sure there was a name for them. So many weird plants had come along over the years, strange hybrids and offshoots, caused by the same thing that caused the zombie plague, or so many claimed. Jay didn't know about such things. That was for smarter men than him to figure out.

All he wanted to do was wrangle zombies and be left alone.

Looked like he'd be wrangling soon enough but the left alone part would be some time in coming.

The ground rose and he spotted a set of small hills ahead. A ways to the right, one of the bushes was flattened as if something had driven over it. Farther in where dirt took over from brush, he spotted tire tracks leading away from the path.

Looked like Thrifty Morris mighta taken a detour.

Jay slowed the truck and turned to follow. His hands tightened on the wheel as the truck bounced underneath his butt. Damn. He was gonna give Thrifty an earful for this. Hell, he'd give Melanie as earful as well. Damn stupid of her to come out here following a wrangler like Thrifty.

His tires spun on the loose dirt, sending up thick clouds of dust before catching and sending him forward. He coughed at the dust that floated through the lip of his window. The seal was a little loose. He'd have to look at fixing it.

A few minutes drive and he spotted a small van in the distance. At least Thrifty had the sense to paint his van beige, allowing it to blend better into the landscape, although the yellow roof didn't work quite so well.

Jay pulled his truck behind the van, turning the engine off and letting the truck coast in close. As it inched forward, he applied the brakes, reducing the dust cloud that formed. Even before the cloud settled, Jay slid on his heavy leather gloves and pulled on his wrangler mask. It covered his head, cheeks and neck in leather and was punched with tiny holes to allow airflow. Even with the holes, it was a hot thing to wear, but it had saved his life many times. He pulled his wide brimmed hat over his head, then grabbed his shotgun. For a moment, he considered adding on the full gear: the chest and back plates, the arm and leg pads, all made from heavy leather, designed to prevent grabbing and biting by the zombies if he was ever caught close up.

And he had been occasionally, caught in a stampede of zombies with only an axe or a club. Those leathers worked magic.

But they were dreadful hot in the desert and he didn't like to put them on until he had to. Best to take a look at the situation first and find Thrifty and Melanie before he suited full up.

He climbed out of the cab and headed for the van. Streaks of dried mud crusted the sides. Thrifty never did care much for his vehicles.

Jay knocked on all the windows but got no response. He didn't really expect one. If Thrifty had been in the van, he woulda stuck his head out as Jay pulled up. They were probably out surveying the herd.

He pushed his glasses up on his face and

studied the ground. There, tracks leading away from the van. Two sets of footprints heading toward those small hills.

Jay followed.

As he crested the small rise, he saw how the long hill plunged down deep off to the left. To the right, it sloped more gently, with jagged crevices and rock for shelter. The prints angled that way, the way he woulda gone. At least Thrifty wasn't that much an idiot to follow the plunge all the way down.

Even from here, he could hear something on the breeze, a sound that could be distant moans and shuffling against sand. He angled toward the right, following the prints but kept his ears listening for those moans. His hand tightened on the shotgun.

He'd rounded an outcropping of a large boulder that loomed over his head when he heard sand shifting in front of him. The shotgun came up in an instant. He crouched and slip slided forward, using the shifting sand as cover. He rounded the boulder, shotgun ready.

"Whoa, watch it there!"

Thrifty held up his thin-fingered hands, gloved in strips of leather. He was a long limbed gawk of a man, more arms and legs than torso. Even his neck was a long thin length that shouldn't be able to carry the melon of his head, but did. He wore the regular outfit of the wrangler: knee high leather boots, heavy leather breastplate and back plate strapped around his thin frame. Strips of heavy leather were tied around his arms and upper legs. His long thin nose overshot his mouth, more a line without lips, and small brown eyes widened beneath his wide brimmed hat.

"Jay, is that you?" he said.

"Yes, it's me, Thrifty."

For a moment, a smile almost crossed his narrow mouth but then it twisted into a frown.

"Hey, this here's my job. I got a contract. Hillard can't be breaking it already. He ain't even given me a chance."

"I'm not here to break your contract," Jay said. "I'm here for Melanie. Where is she?"

"Why you asking?" Thrifty said.

"Murdock asked me to come get her."

"She's learning wrangling," Thrifty said. "She asked me to teach her."

"So you brought her out with a full herd here."

"Twas the way my daddy taught me. You learn quick when a herd's on your tail. Besides, she can tame zombies. I seen it at *Zombee A Go-Go*."

"I seen it too," Jay said. "Ever wonder how she managed to get up on that stage without having to take her clothes off?"

"I don't care," Thrifty said. "She wants to learn wrangling and she's paying for it."

"Paying! You're making her pay?"

"Course," Thrifty said. "I'm a teacher, ain't I? I should be paid for my lessons."

Jay shook his head. "Thrifty, you don't know what you stepped in. Did you bother to ask her who she is?"

"Whadya talking about?" the wrangler said. "She's a zombie tamer."

"She's Murdock's niece," Jay said.

Thrifty's mouth dropped open. "What?"

"That's right. Your little meal ticket is Murdock's niece. Wonder what he'll think if something happens to her or if you decide to take all her money and ditch her in the desert."

"I'd never do that," Thrifty said. "I'm a self respecting wrangler and I'm teachin' her."

"Sure," Jay said. "Where is she? I'll take her out of here before you get in a deeper mess."

A mutinous look spread over Thrifty's face and for a moment Jay thought the wrangler wasn't going to tell him. Great, that was just great. Jay wasn't gonna face Murdock's wrath alone. Heck, he wouldn't face it all. He'd light out for some other place if it came down to it.

'Course that meant he'd never be able to come back around here again.

Then Thrifty's narrow shoulders drooped and he jerked a thumb up past his shoulder.

"She's this way."

He headed off through a narrow break in the rock. The split boulder towered several feet over their heads. As they passed through it, Jay saw a great swath of rubble stretch ahead of them. Huge boulders butted against small ones, others nestling on top of each other as they built up against a cliff wall that sliced deep and low into the desert. It dropped down from where they were into a lower valley maybe half a mile down.

Even from up here, Jay could hear the distant moans and shuffles of zombies down in the valley. From the way the boulders and rock hung over the side, he knew the valley was probably shaded, making it an ideal resting place for zombies. They didn't much like full sun, preferring to attack either at dusk, in full night, or at dawn. If they had to, they'd roam and attack in full day but only if they'd been without prey for a time. Otherwise, daytime was the safest from zombies.

And the best time for wrangling.

Thrifty led him past another huge boulder, deep crevices split into it reflecting red sand in the sunlight, as if the boulder had bled out. Around the edge of the boulder was a narrow rock outcropping that formed a natural platform out over the valley.

Melanie lay on the platform, geared up in zombie wrangling attire. But the leathers she wore still had the sheen of newness and were probably too stiff for proper wear. Silly girl had probably bought 'em special when she'd have been better off with a used set. At least she'd had the sense to tie her long hair back in a braid that wound into a bun clipped to the back of her head.

At the sound of their footsteps sliding on the sand, her head turned. Her dark eyes widened at the sight of Jay standing beside Thrifty. She set down the binoculars she'd been using and rolled over to sit in a cross-legged position.

"What're you doing here?" she said.

"I came to take you back to the *Go-Go*," Jay said. "Your uncle sent me here."

Her lips pressed tight together. A muscle jumped along her jaw. Her shoulders tensed. Her fingers grasping the binoculars whitened.

"I'm not going," she said. "We've got a contract."

"One you didn't negotiate fairly," Jay said. "You didn't tell Thrifty you were Murdock's niece. You didn't mention that little fact to me either."

"It's irrelevant," she said. "I contracted to learn wrangling. Who my uncle is doesn't make any difference." She jerked her chin toward Thrifty. "We have a deal."

"I don't want no trouble," Thrifty said.

He spoke to the platform floor between the two of them. Jay couldn't tell who he was addressing.

"Let's not fuss, Melanie," Jay said. "We're cutting into Thrifty's job here. Let's just go."

"No, I'm not leaving!" She climbed to her feet and moved away from him along the platform.

She glared across the expanse at him. Even from here, he could see the flush of anger on her cheeks and the way it spread down her neck. The leather plate slung too low on her chest, showing too much skin, skin that now flushed in anger. A brief wonder of how far down that flush went flashed through his mind, making his body jerk a little. Damn, keep the mind on the job!

He shifted his shotgun into his left hand and unsnapped a small pouch at his waist. It held the small tranquilizer darts he'd had made up over the years. Perfect for corralling panicked civilians. Sometimes enough of them even took down the occasional zombie, if it was weak enough.

He didn't want to have to use it but he would if he had to.

"Just come along, Melanie."

"You are *not* shooting me with that," she said.

Even in her anger she knew enough to keep her voice low but it didn't matter. A roaring moan sounded from below them.

The herd was on the move.

Damnit.

Thrifty sucked in a startled breath. "They shouldn't be movin' like that!" He slid closer to the edge and peered over.

"Damn if they aren't stampeding! Heading right this way!"

He turned and ran back the way they'd come, his boots kicking up clouds of dust that expanded in the breeze.

Jay held out his hand. "Come on, Melanie, we got to go now."

"It's not my fault," she said. Tears of fury shimmered in her eyes. Her hands tightened into fists, the right one clenching the binoculars.

"Course it's not," Jay said. "Who said it was?"

"They… they all do," she said. "I can't help it. It just happens. That's why I started taming and if I could wrangle too…"

"What are you talkin' about?" Jay said.

"The zombies!" she cried. "They react to me. They follow me. I don't know why and I can't stop it!"

The tears spilled over her cheeks. She swiped a fist at them.

"Whadya you mean they follow you?" he said.

"They always have," she said. "Attacked my parents' settlement when I was a child, followed me when I was sent off to an aunt's. They just won't stop."

"But you learned to tame them," he said. "How do you do that?"

"I don't know," she said. "They just listen to me sometimes. But not enough. Don't you see I need to know how to wrangle."

Jay glanced over the side. Sure enough, zombies were scrabbling forward, clawing over each other as they fought to climb the cliff wall up toward them. The dust from their efforts rose up like smoke, tickling his nose.

"Here's your first lesson of wrangling," he said. "Know when to get out."

Before she could respond, he reached out and grabbed her arm, dragging her back from the edge of the platform. As they hurried away toward the boulder path, Jay glanced back once. A single decaying hand lurched up over the edge of the platform and grabbed hold.

They ran back along the path and this time she didn't argue. Neither bothered with the arrhythmic walk. Now that the zombies knew they were here, a full out run was the only option.

Even with her short legs, Melanie kept up with him, her footsteps pounding double time behind him. Over the dust he caught a whiff of her warm musk. Stray strands of hair came loose from her bun and whipped back from her head. Fortunately not enough for any zombie to grab on to. With zombies, it was every man for himself but Jay wasn't sure he'd be able to leave her behind, and not just because she was Murdock's niece.

Damned if he didn't find himself liking this spitfire of a girl.

They rounded the last boulder and caught sight of his truck. Thrifty's van was long gone, even the dust cloud it must have kicked up had settled. But the pickup truck wasn't alone.

At least a dozen zombies mulled about, a few tapping on the windows but most wandering aimlessly in the dirt. Mouths opened and closed as if chewing or trying to talk. Heads lolled on necks. Bodies swayed back and forth as they lurched on stiff legs. Most were clothed in tattered rags revealing torn flesh that didn't bleed or weep. Two, a man and woman, looked fresh, probably only a few months old, clothing still mostly intact. The woman's long skirt was shredded at the bottom where her shuffling feet had continually stepped on it. The man's shirt was torn at the collar, revealing the shoulder wound that had turned him.

Before she could dart out around him, Jay grabbed Melanie and dragged her back behind the boulder. His back pressed flat against the cold rock. Melanie pressed flat against him, and boy, wasn't that a distraction?

"What is it?" she whispered.

"Zombies near my pickup." He tipped his lips close to her ear to whisper into it. He could feel the stray strands of hair tickle the side of his face. One inhalation and her scent enveloped him. Her body felt so warm and firm against him it was all he could do not to tighten his arm around her.

Boy, did he want to.

"Shouldn't you be concerned about those zombies?" she said.

He caught the curl of a smile at the corner of her mouth. His own smile answered her.

"I reckon you're right."

He moved her back beside him and peered out again to take a better count. Only eleven this time. Still more than he liked to face at once. If that had been the whole herd he'd have no problem shooting them but any gunfire would draw the others. He needed to do it quiet.

Unfortunately, he'd left his clubs and axe in the pickup.

He had an emergency one in the back cab if he could get to it before they jumped him. He just had to wait for the right time. But already he could hear shuffling and moaning coming from back up the path. Zombies had followed them that way. He wouldn't be able to wait for the optimal moment.

Melanie's hand grabbed his arm, staying him before he could rush out.

"Wait," she said. "Let me try to hold them off."

He glanced back at her. "You ever tame so many at once?"

"No," she said. "But I might be able to hold them long enough for you to reach the pickup."

A loud moan behind her made her flinch. Her hand tightened on his arm.

"Please," she said.

"Okay, on a count of three."

He counted, then on three, darted forward. Melanie followed on his heels. He angled wide to the left, around the farthest zombie, an older decaying one that he couldn't tell was a man or boy. It flung its arms out toward him as he passed. Soon the others headed toward him as he aimed for the back of the pickup.

Melanie skidded to a stop in front of the pickup. She held her arms out wide.

"Stop!"

Moans sounded. Heads turned. Feet shuffled. Some took steps toward Melanie, others turned back to where Jay rummaged in the back of the pickup. He pulled out the heavy sword he'd bought from a wrangler down south. He'd only used once or twice, now was time to give it a good test.

The closest zombie had turned to look at it. Jay swung the sword two handed. It sliced true through the air and then clean through the zombie's neck. The body dropped to the ground, spilling out brackish liquid as the head bounced and rolled.

The other zombies stirred as if they realized one of their own had dropped. A few shuffling feet moved toward him.

"Stay!" Melanie's voice called out clear and strong. "To me."

Uh oh, Jay thought. That wasn't a good idea.

Almost as one, the zombies turned toward her. Shuffling steps moved forward. Moans increased in volume.

Uncertainty crossed Melanie's face drawing her eyebrows down and wrinkling her forehead. Her raised arms quivered. Even from here, Jay could see sweat beading along her hairline.

He raised the sword and waded in.

Heads fell as he swung. Bodies dropped to the dust. Moans cut off in mid call. Still none of the others turned to him as he worked. All of them focused on Melanie, moved toward her even as she took small steps backward, fighting to maintain her distance. Sweat now poured down the sides of her face. Her upraised arms shook with strain. Her lips trembled as her teeth clenched.

Jay cut down the last zombie, a male that was heading toward Melanie from the right, its scrabby hands less than a foot from her before Jay swung and sent its head flying. The body dropped in a heap beside her.

Loud moans broke the stillness. From around the boulder behind her, the rest of the zombie hoard poured forth.

Jay grabbed her arm. "Come on!"

They ran for the pickup.

She jumped in the passenger's seat as he slid the sword back into the cab and then climbed into the driver's seat. The engine roared to life. Dust clouds rose up ahead of them, obscuring the zombie crowd as the tires spun. The pickup lurched backward, gaining speed as he accelerated away from the herd.

"Buckle up," Jay said to Melanie, even as he snapped his own seat belt into place. She dragged the belt across her shoulder and belted in.

He spun the wheel. The tires skidded. Dust billowed up. He tasted it as it flooded in through the vents. Beside him, Melanie coughed. He shoved the gear into drive and hit the gas. The wheels spun like mad then caught. The truck leapt forward and raced across the desert floor.

Through the rear view mirror, he watched the herd drop away in the distance. Still he didn't let up on the gas. The zombies had gotten their scent now, both him and Melanie. The zombies would track them as far as they needed to until something else caught their attention.

And with Melanie around, he didn't think anything else'd be catching their attention any time soon.

He kept his hands clenched on the wheel. The truck bounced underneath him. His body felt like it was being shaken into oblivion. All the bones in his arms and legs rattled. He thought his ribs would dislodge and stab into his lungs. Still he didn't let up on the speed. He gave a quick glance to Melanie. Her hands were braced against the dashboard in front of her. He could almost see the slickness of her muscles between the leather pads strapped to her arms.

"You okay?" he said.

Her head twitched toward him. "Yeah."

"They won't stop coming, will they?" he said. "They're coming after you."

He took another look at her and saw her staring at him. Her dark eyes were wide, her usual bravado stripped away to reveal the fear etched into the tiny worry lines around her mouth and eyes. A stray strand of hair fell across her cheek, just to the left of her lips. His fingers itched to brush it back on her head. He could almost feel the softness of her skin.

"You're right," she said. "They won't stop."

Her words faded under the grind of the engine. He nodded. Just as he thought.

He had a couple options. One, to lead the zombies back to Hillard's barn and hope the scent of the people and animals holed up inside would distract the zombies from Melanie. But no self-respecting wrangler could do such a thing, even if he didn't have a contract with Hillard. Jay had claimed to be Thrifty's assistant and so felt bound by that contract, so that option was out.

That only left one choice.

Give the zombies what they want.

But he'd give it to them where he wanted.

The truck bounced on the path and then hit the groves heading back toward the farm. He followed it aways, then spun the wheel to the left, aiming across a flat, empty expanse toward the faint glint of pavement he'd seen. The tires squealed when they caught the cracked pavement and the truck almost seemed to roar louder, as if happy to be on a flatter, denser surface.

Now they really flew. He couldn't see any

dust cloud raised by the zombies, not in the rearview mirror or even over his shoulder. But they were still following. He didn't fool himself.

"Where are we going?" Melanie said.

"Where we're supposed to be going," he said. "Back to *Zombee A Go-Go*."

It took another hour of flat-out racing to reach *Zombee A Go-Go*. He caught sight of the boarded up windows with the painted sign across it. He knew the *Go-Go* had resisted zombie attacks before but he doubted if it had faced a herd this big.

"Stop, you have to stop," Melanie said again. "Let me out!"

"I'll let you out when we reach the *Go-Go*."

"You can't take me there! Not with them following me."

"That's where we're going."

"No, you have to stop! Let me out!"

And so the conversation went around and around for the whole hour.

At one point, she'd tried to jump out of the pickup. She'd undone her buckle and reached for the door handle before he realized what she was up to. Before she could pull it, he hit the child lock, disabling her handle. She tugged at it several times before realizing he'd locked her in.

Then she'd started with the "let me out."

She'd tried crying, threatening, cajoling, but he held fast in the face of all of it, and didn't it just kill him a little inside to say no to her. There was something inside him that just wanted to say yes, yes to anything for her.

Was it the same for the zombies?

He reckoned maybe it was.

His tires spun as he swerved to a stop before the front door of *Zombee A Go-Go*. Melanie had her hand on the door handle again. She looked at him expectantly.

"You just wait here," he said.

He slipped out before she opened her mouth to speak. He hit the lock and then doubled locked it with his remote. Melanie lunged across the driver's side and tugged at the door. It stayed firmly shut. Her fist pounded on the window. She yelled at him, her voice garbled inside the truck but he imagined those words weren't all that friendly.

He rushed into the *Go-Go*, impatiently enduring the decontamination before he could step into the bar proper. The late lunch crowd was just finishing. He spotted Morton, Kowalski, Strainer and even Breaydon over by the stage. Good. The more the better.

Bertha was still on shift and approached Jay, wiping her hands on a white towel. "Need a table, Jay?"

"Where's Murdock?" he said. "We've got an emergency."

"He's back in the office," she said.

"Get him."

She nodded and hurried off even as

Kowalski stepped forward. He held a beer in one beefy hand, the other hooked into the belt loop of his faded leather pants. A faded jean jacket stretched across his shoulders and just managed to cover his ample stomach. He took a sip of his beer and didn't bother to wipe the foam from his grey mustache.

"What's up, Jay?"

Jay debated telling him or waiting for Murdock. Every moment counted. As he opened his mouth, he spotted Murdock entering the dining room from the narrow doorway leading to his back office. He nodded toward Murdock.

"If you'll wait a sec I can tell ya all at once," he said.

"You bet," Kowalski said. Then he wiped the foam from his mustache.

Murdock reached them. "Did you find her?"

"She's out in the truck but we got a real problem," Jay said.

"What's that?"

"The biggest zombie herd I ever seen is headed this way," Jay said. "It's got her scent and ain't giving it up."

Kowalski scowled as Murdock frowned.

"Big enough to take the *Go-Go*?" Murdock said.

Jay nodded. "Think so."

Murdock clapped a hand on Jay's shoulder. "Let's get Melanie."

Jay led him back out to the pickup truck. Melanie was still trapped inside the front cab but she'd managed to pry open the glove compartment and was trying to use a screwdriver from it to pick the lock. At the sight of Jay and Murdock, she started yelling again and waving the screwdriver. Jay didn't want to face that screwdriver, but he pulled out the remote and unlocked the door. She tumbled out, righting herself before Murdock could grab her.

"You son of a bitch!" she shouted at Jay.

"Settle down, Melanie." Murdock tightened his hand on her shoulder. "I told Jay to bring you back."

"Did you tell him to make sure I led a herd of zombies here to destroy the place too?" she said.

"We'll take care of those zombies," Murdock said.

"Really? How many wranglers are here? A hundred? You'll need that many for the zombies that are coming." Her voice hitched in her throat. Her face twitched. Jay could tell she was fighting back tears again but from fear or frustration he didn't know.

"They're coming for me, uncle," she finally managed to say.

"Well, they aren't gettin' you," Murdock said.

She shook her head. "No, I won't let everyone here die in my place."

"We got no intention of that," Jay said.

Melanie shrugged off Murdock's hand and

got in Jay's face. Without her high boots, she barely came up to his chin but her face lifted, looking up at him. He could smell her sweat, dust, and desperation all mixed into a heady scent that made him dizzy. It was all he could do to focus on her words and not just watch the way her lips moved.

"What do you think is going to happen?" she said. "Those zombies won't stop until they get me, even if that means going through idiots like you!"

Jay shook his head, forcing himself to focus, damnit, focus on anything other than the way her chest heaved as she tried to rein in her anger.

"Excuse me but it seems that'll help us in the long run. I saw how focused they was on gettin' to you. They didn't even notice me. We get enough wranglers, we might just be able to take 'em all out."

"Might," she said. "They focused like that only because I was calling them. I can't keep that up and once I slip they'll notice you. That'll be it."

"We ain't got much choice," Jay said. He clamped his hand around her slim wrist. "You ain't goin' nowhere."

"No!" she said, but Murdock stepped forward and grabbed her other arm. They dragged her through the door of *Zombee A Go-Go*.

Murdock threw her through the decontamination chamber and caught her on the other side.

"Gents, we got a herd of zombies on the way. Send out a call to protect the *Go-Go*," Murdock said. "About how long we got, Jay?"

"No more than forty-five minutes," Jay said.

"Be back here in half an hour," Murdock said. "Bring what reinforcements you can. This'll be the biggest wrangle in history, gentlemen."

Excited murmurs spread through the

room. Jay almost grinned but stopped himself. Murdock sure knew how to sell this to a bunch of wranglers. If they got out of this alive, the survivors would have the biggest bragging rights in the county, heck maybe even the whole country. They'd be legends. They'd be heroes.

They'd be the ultimate zombie wranglers.

The men streamed out through the front door, hurrying to fetch any and all fellow wranglers within a half hour's distance. Jay stayed behind. No way was he letting Melanie out of his sight.

Murdock seemed to understand. He made some comment about getting the girls in the back sorted and stepped away. Melanie sat at one of the tables, shoulders drooping. Jay sat in the chair next to her, not sure he wanted to be in range if she struck out but wanting to be nearby if she made a run for it.

Not that she looked like she was going to. More flyaway hair coiled out from her braid, sticking out in all directions. Tears and sweat had smudged dirt on her face. Her leathers didn't look quite so new anymore but still looked a bit stiff. Her expression held more displeasure with him than anyone ever had since his momma.

"How'd you know you could tame the zombies?" he said.

"What?" she said.

"They attacked your parents and followed you to your aunt's," he said. "How'd you know you could tame 'em?"

"I had to do something to stop them," she said. "They followed me, I thought they might listen to me."

"So what is it you're tellin' them to do," he said, "when you're on stage with 'em?"

Her head tilted at him. "What? Why do you want to know that?"

"Just answer," he said.

"I'm telling them to do what I want: sit in the chair, catch the ball. What does that have to do with anything?"

"I'm just wondering if you could do the same thing with that herd coming this way."

A harsh laugh burst from her mouth.

"Are you kidding me? I can't hold back that big a herd. You saw I could barely hold back that small group that attacked us."

"Not hold 'em back," he said. "What if you told them to do something, anything else? Just enough to confuse 'em, distract 'em for us."

She shook her head. "I don't know."

"Listen, these wranglers are coming back to fight that herd. You can either help us or not, but we'll be fightin' whatever ya do. It just might help if you did what you claim you can do."

That done it. Her shoulders pulled back as she bristled. The regular flash of anger flared in her eyes as she sat up straight.

"After what you saw, you still don't believe me?"

He shrugged. "Coulda all be coincidence."

"Don't think I don't know what you're doing, Jay," she said. "You think if you make me angry enough I won't be scared."

He shrugged. "Is it working?"

"I'm angry enough to kick your ass."

A yell sounded from outside. Jay pushed back from the table to stand up.

"Tell ya what. We survive this, you'll get your chance."

"Don't think I won't do it," she said.

"No, ma'am," he said. "I'm countin' on it."

The corners of her mouth twitched but she kept her lips shut tight. He took her arm and steered her toward Murdock's office.

"Get into the interior of the building. Stay away from the windows."

She pulled her arm from his grasp. "No, I have to get to the roof."

"You can't be up there."

"I have to," she said. "I have to be able to see them. If you want me to try taming them, I have to see them."

He didn't like the idea of her exposed but it wasn't like the zombies would be shooting anything. The highest section of the roof of *Zombee A Go-Go* was three stories high. If she stayed there, maybe it would be okay.

Murdock stepped out from back stage, leading five of the dancers. Two of the women held high powered rifles, the others carried boxes of ammunition.

"Take those stairs," he said, gesturing toward the side door. The women hurried across to climb the stairs.

"You go with them," Jay said to Melanie.

"Wait a minute," Murdock said. "She's not going up there."

"I have to," Melanie said. "I have to see the zombies if I'm going to do anything."

"You can't tame that many, girl," Murdock said. "I'll not have you up there putting yourself in danger."

"Maybe I should take her out wrangling then," Jay said.

Murdock's face reddened. "Get upstairs."

Melanie followed the women.

"I'll help with the fortifications outside," Jay said.

He hurried away before Murdock could reply.

He stepped outside and was helping Kowalski haul across the secondary steel barrier when a low rumble sounded on the horizon. Jay sniffed the air. Over the ever-present scent of dust, he caught the first whiff of zombie decay. Dark shapes shifted on the horizon, spreading across like a stain.

The shiver that ran up his spine wasn't caused by the sudden gust of wind.

"Geez, is that them?" Kowalski said.

"That's them," Jay said. "Let's suit up."

As they rotated through getting ready and pulling out more barriers around *Zombee A Go-Go*, more and more wranglers appeared, arriving from all directions by ones and twos. Most hauled out axes or swords, some carried bats with spikes in the ends. One even had a samurai sword. All wore variations of the wrangler outfit: leather padding with space for movement and masks to protect breathing. Jay lost count after twenty.

He'd never seen so many wranglers out for a fight at once. As he clutched his own sword, seeing 'em all made him stand a little taller.

The herd spread out almost as far as he could see. It looked like a dark mass of moving bodies, all lurching and lunging forward. The steady moans and wails drifted toward the *Go-Go*, sounding like the wail of hell itself.

Jay took a look around at the various barriers. Stretches of steel wiring and fencing, several concrete barriers, smaller walls of stone and brick, all set at various intervals and distances from the *Go-Go*. Zombies weren't known for their coordination so anything that got in the way could impede them, at least long enough for a wrangler to cut their heads off or crush their skulls.

He lifted his hand to shade his eyes and looked up to the roof of the *Go-Go*. He thought he saw a glint up there, maybe a reflection off the barrel of one of the rifles. He hoped those girls were good shots and didn't end up shooting a wrangler.

No matter how hard he looked, he couldn't see Melanie.

Then the moaning got louder, and he didn't have time to think.

The first wave came slow, almost leisurely, as if they were waiting for the wranglers to come pick them off. Morton and Kowalski waded out, tag teaming and slicing as they went. Jay followed up with another two wranglers, Stenson and Brommel. They cut across the end, isolating a group of zombies. The zombies floundered, turning in circles, as if unsure where to go. Strainer and Braeydon rushed over, taking them down.

Was that twenty, thirty zombies down? Jay couldn't be sure. They seemed to move slower than usual, without focus. He'd never seen zombies move that way. Then he paused.

Of course.

Melanie.

He risked a look up. Now he caught a glimpse of her, standing at the edge of the roof. Her arms outstretched. Then her hips began to move from side to side, swiveling. Her hands beckoned.

And the zombies followed suit.

That was when the music started.

Murdock must have aimed the speakers right out the windows because the music blasted out of the *Go-Go* like a flare. Suddenly zombies surged forward. Arms waved disjointedly. Bodies lurched and tried to swivel. Knees buckled as hips thrust out to the side. Heads were thrown back, making it even easier to cut them off or bash them in.

On the roof, Melanie danced away. She'd even undone her hair and let it fly free, whipping up around her head in a flurry. Her body moved and swayed to the music. She didn't have the polish of the regular *Go-Go* dancers but Jay had to force himself to look away from her gyrating body.

Man, his leathers felt tight all of a sudden.

Around him, the zombies jerked and lunged in a horrific parody of Melanie's dance. They seemed oblivious to the wranglers moving through them. Within the span of a dance song, the largest, most dangerous herd of zombies Jay'd ever seen had turned into the easiest. One song finished and clicked to the next. Melanie continued dancing and the zombies followed her lead while the wranglers took them down, one after the other.

It took the entire group of twenty-three wranglers almost two hours to finish the last of the herd.

Jay took the final zombie down with a backhand swing of his sword. It caught the head of the male zombie as it wiggled its shoulders in a gross parody of trying to shimmy. Jay's sword got caught in the back of the zombie's skull. He had to jerk several times really hard before the sword came out, spraying a brackish liquid from the zombie's brain.

The zombie moaned and faltered but didn't fall completely.

Jay reversed the sword and swung again, this time slicing through the male's neck. Now the head went flying, bouncing and rolling to a stop several feet away. The body twitched as if unwilling to give up the dance, then collapsed into the dust.

Jay wiped his hand across his forehead and looked around.

Dust floated in the air, creating an almost fog effect, softening the image of heaps of bodies piled on the ground and stretching as far as he could see around *Zombee A Go-Go*. The smell of dust and decay coated the insides of his nostrils and seemed to seep into his body with every breath. Would he ever get rid of the taste of it, the smell of it? His muscles ached, especially his shoulders from swinging the sword. He'd never killed so many zombies at one time and it had never been so easy.

The thumping music switched off. In the ensuing silence, Jay listened to the heavy breaths of the other wranglers. Everyone was doing what he was doing, stretching arms, rotating heads, groaning as they cracked their backs.

The door of the *Go-Go* opened and Murdock stepped out. Behind him, the girls clustered in the doorway, peering out. Jay even saw Bertha looking out with her mouth open in a big O.

But he didn't see Melanie.

He glanced up to the roof.

She was gone from there too.

"Gentlemen, I don't know how I can rightly thank you for protecting *Zombee A Go-Go*," Murdock said. His voice seemed to boom out across the expanse of zombie corpses.

"Unfortunately, the job isn't done yet. We need to get rid of these bodies. We've got a zombie pit out back. It's time to create the biggest zombie bonfire in history. And after that, boys, everything's on the house tonight."

Jay was too tired to cheer but a few of the other wranglers made noises of approval. Kowalski nodded, a big grin on his face. Morton clapped his hands.

"Let's burn these bones, boys," Murdock said.

The cleanup took longer than the fight. Wasn't that always the way.

Jay figured his momma woulda been surprised after all of her grousing how he kept his room at home to see how often he had to engage in clean up. Maybe this was his penance for always talking back to his momma.

Finally they managed to drag the bodies into a huge pile over a hundred feet away from the *Go-Go*.

The girls stood in a row circling the side nearest the *Go-Go*. They carried extinguishers in their hands with several stockpiled behind them.

The wranglers managed to toss the bodies into a pile over fifteen feet high. The pile stretched out for what felt like miles to Jay, but he was just tired. His sense of proportion was right gone now. He kept glancing back at the girls, hoping to catch a glimpse of Melanie, but she didn't appear.

Probably resting after her taming dance, he thought.

As they tossed the last of the corpses onto the pile and the sun began setting in the distance, Murdock stepped up.

He sprayed lighter fluid onto the pile as high as he could reach. He handed the canister back to one of the girls and picked up a small dented flamethrower. He paused with his thick finger on the trigger and then turned to the assembled group of dusty, sweaty, worn-out wranglers and the staff of the *Go-Go*, all dancers, wait staff and cooks standing with arms crossed in front, respectful.

"We wouldn't have survived this day without all of you fighting together," Murdock said. "This is the biggest herd I've ever seen and we can proud of what we accomplished today. Every one of you did an outstanding job. I am mighty grateful. All your names will be forever remembered at the *Go-Go*."

"What about Melanie?" Jay said. His voice cut across the space between them. "We wouldna been able to do any of it without her taming."

Some of the wranglers murmured around him. He could hear the scoffing in their tones. He whirled on them.

"Shut up!" he said. "You don't know nothing. That girl tamed those zombies like nobodies' business. Anybody here get bit? Anybody here even get swatted? I ain't never heard of such a thing. Sure it was work taking down all them zombies but we barely had to fight, just stroll on through and take 'em down, and all because of Melanie the zombie tamer!"

The murmurs stopped and he saw heads nodding in agreement. He turned back to Murdock, who was smiling as he held the flamethrower.

"I say Melanie should be the one to start the fire," Jay said. "She earned it."

Now the murmurs behind him supported that idea.

"I agree," Murdock said.

He set the flamethrower down on the ground and crossed to the back door of the *Go-Go*. A few moments later he reemerged, supporting Melanie. She stumbled forward. Her body seemed to sag as she moved. Her head dipped forward. Her long dark hair hung in a tattered curtain across her shoulders, obscuring her face. Murdock draped her left arm over his shoulder as he helped her. Her right hand hung down at her side, flopping as if it wasn't even attached to her body.

Before he knew what he was doing, Jay moved to take hold of her right hand and arm, helping to support her until they reached the flamethrower. Over her head, Jay caught a glimpse of Murdock's face tilted toward him, eyes narrowed in suspicion. Jay ignored it. He leaned down to pick up the flamethrower and pressed it into Melanie's right hand.

"Melanie, I don't know much about most things, but I do know about zombies," Jay said. "And I ain't ever seen better zombie fighting that what you did today."

She lifted her head. Dark circles hung under her eyes. Weariness etched across her face. Her skin was pale and washed out. Even her lips looked colorless. But a twinkle of interest burned in her eyes.

"What are you talking about?" she said. "I didn't fight the zombies. I couldn't even stop them from moving."

"You fought 'em all right," he said. "Not one of us got bit or hurt. You had 'em dancing and ignoring us." He smiled. "You made it easy for us."

"I did? I saw them keep moving."

"They were dancing, following you."

Her eyes widened. He could almost see the energy flow back into her. He felt her straighten beside him. "They were?"

He nodded. "Sure were. But they don't dance near as well as you."

A smile lit up her face. Her hand tightened on the flamethrower. She pressed her cheek against his and he inhaled deep, breathing in the musk of her scent. It made him dizzy.

"If you thought that dancing was good, I'll show you what I'm even better at later." Her voice purred in his ear.

His mouth went dry. Her lips brushed against his cheek as she pulled away and turned to face the pile. She lifted the flamethrower.

"Rest in peace," she said and hit the trigger. Flame sprayed out catching the pile and flashing upward. Soon the flames engulfed the pile and rose into the early evening air.

Melanie took Jay's hand.

"Walk me back in?" she said. "I think we could use a good washing up."

"Yes, ma'am," he said. They shuffled back to the *Go-Go*, leaving the others to watch the rising flames. Jay held the door for her and let her pass before him.

"We'll have to shower together," Melanie said as she walked by him. "Have to preserve water."

He swallowed. "Yes, ma'am."

Damn, sometimes this leather was too damn tight.

She smiled and took his hand to lead him into the back.

About the Author

Based in Toronto, Canada, Rebecca M. Senese writes horror, science fiction and mystery/crime, often all at once in the same story. Garnering an Honorable Mention in "The Year's Best Science Fiction" and nominated for numerous Aurora Awards, her work has appeared in *Tesseracts 16: Parnassus Unbound, Tesseracts 15: A Case of Quite Curious Tales, Ride the Moon, TransVersions, Deadbolt Magazine, On Spec, The Vampire's Crypt, Storyteller, Reflection's Edge, Future Syndicate* and *Into the Darkness*, amongst others.

When not serving up tales of the macabre, mysterious or wondrous, she volunteers as a zombie or vampire at haunted attractions in October to stalk and scare all the unsuspecting innocents.

Find Me Online

Website - http://www.RebeccaSenese.com
Twitter - http://twitter.com/RebeccaSenese